For Louis, Zach, and Stella x
R. Q.
For Granny Jean
A. F.

First U.S. edition 2018

Library of Congress Catalog Card Number pending
ISBN 978-0-7636-9952-9

18 19 20 21 22 23 WKT 10 9 8 7 6 5 4 3 2 1

Printed in Shenzhen, Guangdong, China

This book was typeset in Juste.
The illustrations were done in mixed media.

Nosy Crow
an imprint of
Candlewick Press
99 Dover Street
Somerville, Massachusetts 02144

www.nosycrow.com
www.candlewick.com

Mr. & Mrs.
Burrow

Anna   Adelaide

Betsy   Bill

THAT BEAR CAN'T BABYSIT

Casper   Clive

Dotty

Ruth Quayle
Alison Friend

An imprint of Candlewick Press

Mr. and Mrs. Burrow had a lot of children.
There was Anna and Adelaide, Betsy and Bill, Casper and Clive,
and there was little Dotty, too.

Most of the time, everything was just fine, but one
Friday, an invitation arrived and, well, things got a bit tricky.

"Oooh!" said Mrs. Burrow. "A party!"
Then she looked at her children.
"Oh, dear," she said. "We can't possibly go."

"We can," said Mr. Burrow. "We'll get a babysitter."

BABYSITTER WANTED FOR 7 BUNNIES

They put up a sign,
but nobody called.
Nobody knocked.
Nobody lined up outside.
Well, nobody except . . .

Bear.

Bear did not have a fancy suit.
He did not have shiny shoes.
And he was a bit . . . large.

"That bear can't babysit,"
said Mrs. Burrow with a gulp.

But they were going to be late
for the party, so that bear
would have to do.

Mr. and Mrs. Burrow flung on their best clothes, crossed their fingers, and waved good-bye.

"What should we do?" asked Bear.
"Shall I read you a story?"

"Actually," said Anna politely, "we can read
by ourselves. We like to read scary stories."

"Is that allowed?" asked Bear.

Adelaide smiled. "Oh, yes. Mom and Dad **always** let us read *The Bunny Beast.*"

"Really?" said Bear.

"Yes, **always**," said Anna and Adelaide, winking at each other.

"Once in a dark forest lived the Bunny Beast," whispered Adelaide. "He hid behind trees and waited for baby rabbits to hop past. Then he sharpened his claws. . . ."

The bunnies were scared. They pulled their ears over their eyes. Anna and Adelaide began to cry.

"We shouldn't have read that book," wailed Anna and Adelaide.

"That bear can't babysit!"

"Oh, dear," said Bear. "Perhaps we should eat something."

"We'll cook," said Betsy.

"Is that allowed?" asked Bear.

"Oh, yes," said Bill. "Mom and Dad always let us make supper."

"Really?" said Bear.

"Yes, always," said Betsy and Bill, winking at each other.

Betsy and Bill prepared
a yummy supper of
178 pieces of candy,
seven helpings of ice cream,
thirty-six cookies, and
a big jar of chocolate spread.

Then they all felt **very** sick.

"We shouldn't have eaten that food," moaned Betsy and Bill.

"That bear can't babysit!"

"Oh, dear," said Bear. "Perhaps some fresh air would make you feel better."

Casper and Clive ran straight for the hose.

"Is that allowed?" asked Bear.

"Oh, yes," said Casper, nudging Clive. "Mom and Dad always let us water the garden."

"Really?" said Bear.

"Yes, always," said Casper and Clive, winking at each other.

Casper and Clive squirted the hose at Betsy and Bill.
Betsy and Bill threw a bucket of water at
Anna and Adelaide, and Anna and Adelaide
poured the watering can over Casper and Clive.

Everyone was wet, cold, and miserable.

"We shouldn't have played with the hose!" cried Casper and Clive.

"That bear can't babysit.

That bear is hopeless.

That bear is—

"Bear, what are you doing?"

"Oh!" said Bear. "I'm building a ship.
I'm going on an adventure."

"Wait!" said the bunnies.
"Can we come, too?"

They helped Bear build a ship
with room for everyone, even Dotty.

Then they set sail and forgot
to feel cold or miserable.

They'd been exploring for nearly
twenty-seven whole minutes when Bear
let down the anchor and jumped ashore.

"Bear," said Betsy and Bill,
"where are you going?"

"All adventurers need something to eat," said Bear.

"Wait!" called the bunnies. "Can we come, too?"

They dug up crunchy carrots, sweet beets, and spicy radishes. The bunnies ate until their tummies were full, and no one felt sick at all.

By then, it was dark.

"I can hear something in the trees," said Anna.

"What if it's the Bunny Beast?" said Adelaide.

"We're scared!" cried the bunnies.
And they pulled their ears down over their eyes.

But then Bear said, "Maybe
I should read a story now.
Once upon a time, there
was a family of sleepy
little bunnies. . . ."

One by one, the bunnies gathered around Bear.
And one by one, they fell fast asleep.

By the time Mr. and Mrs. Burrow came home, all the bunnies were tucked in bed.

"Well, Bear!" said Mrs. Burrow. "How were the bunnies?"

Bear smiled. "They were a delight," he said.

"Really?" asked Mr. Burrow.

The bunnies peeked out from under their covers.

"Yes," said Bear, smiling.

Mr. and Mrs. Burrow smiled as Bear shuffled home.

"Well," said Mrs. Burrow,
"that bear **can** babysit."

"Yes," said Mr. Burrow.
"Six little bunnies, safe and sound."

Mrs. Burrow gulped.
"Wait a minute," she said.
"Did you say **six**?"

"Seven little bunnies, safe and sound!"

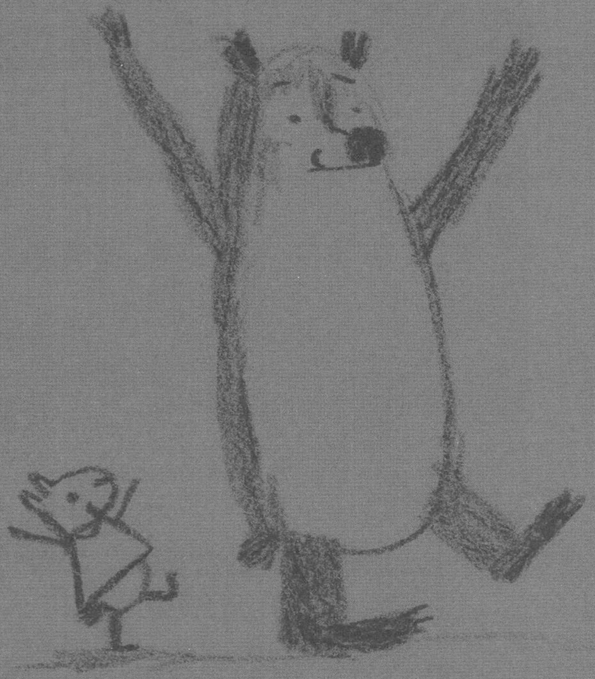

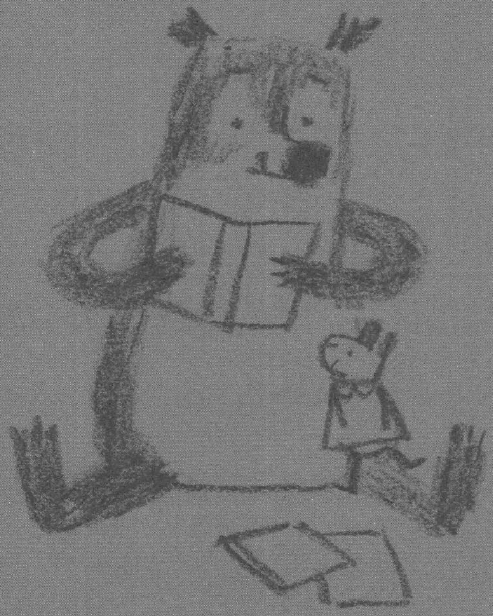